LOOK AND FIND®

Disney
PIRATES of the CARIBBEAN
AT WORLD'S END

Illustrated by Art Mawhinney and
the Disney Storybook Artists

Based on the screenplay written by Ted Elliott & Terry Rossio
Based on the characters created by Ted Elliott & Terry Rossio and
Stuart Beattie and Jay Wolpert
Based on Walt Disney's Pirates of the Caribbean
Produced by Jerry Bruckheimer
Directed by Gore Verbinski

Published by Louis Weber, C.E.O., Publications International, Ltd.
7373 North Cicero Avenue, Lincolnwood, Illinois 60712

Ground Floor, 59 Gloucester Place, London W1U 8JJ

Customer Service: 1-800-595-8484 or customer_service@pilbooks.com

www.pilbooks.com

p i kids is a registered trademark of Publications International, Ltd.

Look and Find is a registered trademark of
Publications International, Ltd., in the United States and in Canada.

Manufactured in USA.

8 7 6 5 4 3 2 1

ISBN-13: 978-1-4127-8019-3
ISBN-10: 1-4127-8019-5

 publications international, ltd.

Elizabeth Swann finds herself in Singapore, far from her home of Port Royal. But she still manages to blend right in. Look for Miss Swann, then find the rest of the pirates, and Tia Dalma, with whom Swann may be forced to form an uneasy alliance.

Elizabeth

Gibbs

Pintel

Ragetti

Tia Dalma

Tai Huang

Barbossa

In an effort to find and rescue Jack Sparrow, the *Hai Peng* was destroyed when it sailed over the edge of the world. Look around the sands of Davy Jones's Locker to find these bits of flotsam.

Oriental ginger jar

Fan

Sheathed bayonet

Book

Tea pot

Woven basket

Crate

The answer to the ancient riddle really rocked the boat! While the *Black Pearl* is keelside-up, look for these things that are upside-down.

Chicken

Jug

Candelabra

Britches

Bucket of tar

Pineapple

Crate

Parrot

Sao Feng has captured Elizabeth. Elizabeth wasn't taken easily, though. Look around the ship to see who has suffered at her hands.

"Who among you do you name Captain?" demands Davy Jones, as his crew swarms the beleaguered *Empress*. Look for these surprised pirates who never expected Elizabeth to be the captain!

As the Brethren Court convenes, pirates from around the world drop anchor in Shipwreck Cove. As the *Black Pearl* makes its way to Shipwreck City, look for these vessels that hail from distant waters.

Dhow

Fusta

Schooner

Barque

Flyboat

Carrack

Sloop

While we watch and wait to see who produces the Pieces of Eight, look around the chamber to find these other eights.

Knot

8 of spades

Pocket watch

Silver coin

Carved 8

A mangy cat

Serpent tattoo

The wrath of Calypso is unleashed at last! Can you find these poor pirates who are nearly engulfed by the skittering tidal wave of claws?

Ragetti

Jack

Pintel

Will

Barbossa

Elizabeth

Tia Dalma's organ grinder isn't the only animal out and about in the harbor tonight. Can you find these?

Yellow canary

Snake

Rat

Monkey

Parrot

Pig

Rooster

Cat

It appears the *Black Pearl* will have a pair of captains—Jack Sparrow and Barbossa. See if you can find these other pairs of items washed up on shore.

Spectacles

Boots

Lovebirds

Earrings

Dice

Pears

Britches

The riddle that helps Jack and his crew escape the Locker mentions a mysterious flash of green. Look around the upside-down *Black Pearl* for these other green things.

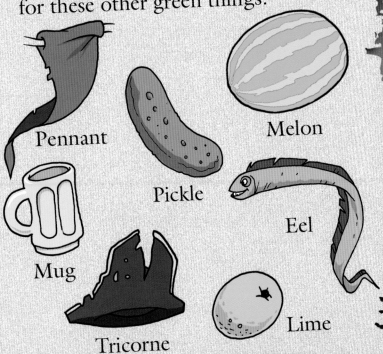

Pennant

Melon

Pickle

Mug

Eel

Tricorne

Lime

The Chinese crew will need to learn the ropes of their newly captured English vessel. Check the lines and riggings for these knots they'll need to know.

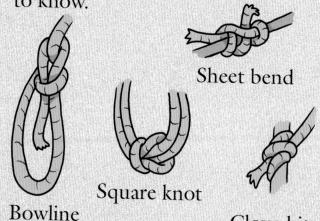

Sheet bend

Bowline

Square knot

Clove hitch

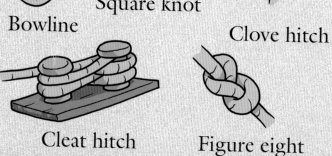

Cleat hitch

Figure eight

Elizabeth needs a few things as captain of the *Empress*. Can you find the items Elizabeth might require?

Keys

Logbook

Spyglass

Blunderbuss

Rolled-up map

Sextant

Cutlass

Every pirate has his—or her—own Jolly Roger. Look around Shipwreck Cove to find these different pirate flags.

Dueling skulls

Laughing skull

Dancing skeleton

Winged hourglass

Broken heart

Angel skull

Skull and crossed swords

If the Brethren Court votes to release Calypso, the high seas will be wild again—perfect for some old-fashioned treachery. There are 12 concealed daggers in the room. Can you find them all?

Ten thousand crabs? That's a lot of shells! Go back to the *Black Pearl* to find these other shells on board.

Whelk shell

Snail shell

Scallop shell

Oyster shell

Periwinkle shell

Conch shell